INTERFACT™

THE BOOK AND DISK THAT WORK TOGETHER

WATER

TWO CAN™

PRINCETON ■ LONDON

Book and disk by
act-two Ltd

Published in the United States and Canada by
Two-Can Publishing LLC
234 Nassau Street
Princeton, NJ 08542

For information on other Two-Can books and multimedia,
Call 1-609-921-6700, fax 1-609-921-3349, or visit our web site at
http://www.two-canpublishing.com

ISBN: 1-58728-469-3

2 4 6 8 10 9 7 5 3 1

Photographic Credits: All photographs are ©Fiona Pragoff, except for the following:
Front cover Cosmo Condina/ Tony Stone Images; p.8 (top and bottom right) Science Photo Library,
(bottom left) Pictor International; p.9 ZEFA Picture Library (UK) Ltd; p.12 Oxford Scientific Films, (inset)
Frank Lane Picture Agency Ltd; p.13 (top and bottom) Ardea, (centre) Frank Lane Picture Agency Ltd;
p.14 ZEFA Picture Library (UK) Ltd; p.16 Bruce Coleman Ltd; p.22 ZEFA Picture Library (UK) Ltd; p.23
(top) ZEFA Picture Library (UK) Ltd; p.25 Bruce Coleman Ltd; p.28 Ardea; p.29 (top) Bruce Coleman Ltd,
(bottom) Ardea; p.32, 33 Tony Stone Images.

Thanks to the staff and pupils of St Thomas C.E. Primary School, London W10 and also to
Pippa West and Lucy Davis.

Printed in Hong Kong by Wing King Tong

INTERFACT

THE BOOK AND DISK THAT WORK TOGETHER

Dive into **INTERFACT**, the book and disk that's oceans of fun and awash with facts!

● **The disk is packed with interactive games, puzzles, quizzes, and activities that are challenging, fun, and full of interesting facts.**

Play Wash Out and give Muddy Mike a much-needed bath.

What percentage of a chicken is water?

CHECK

Floating and sinking

Have you ever noticed that some things **float** and some things **sink**? Make a collection of things from around the house and guess which ones will float and which ones will sink.

▼ Fill a tank or bucket with water. Put your collection of things in the water. Were you surprised? Did you think that the heavy things would sink and the light ones float?

something that floats. You have to push to make it go underwater. How long does it take to rise up to the surface again?

▼ Fill a balloon or see-through polythene bag with water. Tell a friend that you can make it weigh nothing! Push the balloon under the water. It does not float or sink because it contains water, and so weighs the same as the water around it.

DISK LINK Take the plunge! Discover more materials that float or sink in SINK OR SWIM.

● **Open the book and discover more fascinating information highlighted with lots of full-color illustrations and photographs.**

Read about simple water experiments you can try at home.

● To get the most out of **INTERFACT**, use the book and disk together. Look out for the special signs, called Disk Links and Bookmarks. To find out more, turn to page 41.

41

BOOKMARK

DISK LINK
Dip in and discover more materials that float or sink in SINK OR SWIM.

Once you've clicked on to **INTERFACT**, you'll never look back.

LOAD UP!
Go to **page 39** to find out how to load your disk and click into action.

What's on the disk

HELP SCREEN

Learn how to use the disk in no time at all.

INTERFACT

WATER

To take a look at the activities on the disk, click the underlined arrow keys with your mouse.

As you do this, you'll see a description of each activity in the reading box.

Click on the picture at the top of the screen to select the activity you want to investigate.

And remember! Any words underlined like this are hot. Touch them with your mouse for more information.

These are the controls the Help Screen will tell you how to use:
- arrow keys
- reading boxes
- "hot" words

THIRSTY WORK

Race around the water cycle with tour guide, Thirsty Kirsty!

How do trees take in water?

Take a trip from the sea, up to the clouds, downstream to the city, and back again! You'll need lots of water for the journey, but watch out, or Thirsty Kirsty will drink it all!

WASH OUT

Can you figure out where all the water's gone before the plug is pulled?

What percentage of a chicken is water?

CHECK

It's bathtime for Muddy Mike, but you need to brush up on your water knowledge or be a washout! Clean up in this test on water's whereabouts!

SINK OR SWIM

Get dunking with Claude and Shelly's floating and sinking game!

Some objects that look heavier than water may float because they are hollow.

Why do some materials float and others sink? Figure it out, then play the guessing game with two keen marine collectors.

UNDER PRESSURE

Have you got what it takes to be a deep-sea troubleshooter?

The Special Submergency Services are looking for new recruits. Do you have the skills they need? Get suited up and dive, dive, dive on all kinds of exciting underwater missions.

ALL ABOARD

Take the wheel of your own fleet of cargo ships!

Get on board as a cargo ship captain and discover how ships float on the sea. Load up at the docks, but don't choose too heavy a cargo or you could be sunk!

EVERY DROP COUNTS

Wise up and become a water saver at home.

It takes 24 gallons of water to fill a bathtub.

Do you know how much water you and your family use around the house? Fill in your personal water profile and learn how you can save water, too!

FIRE-FIGHTER

Put out a blaze in this wild water knowledge test.

911 Emergency! A house is in flames and you have been called to the scene to put it out. Answer questions on the world of water to keep the fire at bay!

What's in the book

*All words in the text that appear in **bold** can be found in the glossary*

Water over the world

Water is all around us. It covers most of the earth, and all living things need it to survive. We have to drink plenty of it every day. Our bodies are made up of about two-thirds water!

Water first appeared on the earth thousands of millions of years ago as a gas that burst out of volcanoes. This gas, called **water vapor**, cooled down to form the **oceans**. Now water can easily be found as a liquid, a gas, and solid **ice**. Look around and see how many places you can find water in all its different forms. Then discover its amazing properties.

▼ Most of the water on the earth is seawater, which is too salty for us to drink. This water is home to millions of living things. These range from tiny animals and plants called plankton that float near the surface, to the earth's largest mammals, the blue whales that feed on them.

▲ When liquid water is **boiled**, it turns into a gas called **steam**.

▼ When water freezes, it turns into solid ice like these icicles.

▼ There are about 53,000 trillion cubic feet (1,500 million cubic meters) of water on the earth. Water in the form of ice has even been found in deep craters on the moon!

DISK LINK
Discover how much water there is around you in WASH OUT.

The water cycle

condensation

rain

streams

rivers

evaporation

sea

The earth's water is hardly ever still. Water from the sea travels on a long journey called the **water cycle**. As seawater is warmed up by **energy** from the sun, it **evaporates**, turning to **water vapor** that **condenses** to form clouds. When it rains, this water flows into rivers, **lakes,** and **oceans**. Then the cycle begins again.

◀ You can see the water cycle in action in your home. Pour a little water onto a plate. Leave it overnight. In the morning, the water level has dropped a little. Where has the water gone? It has turned from liquid water into water vapor in the air.

DISK LINK
Would you like to take a trip around the water cycle? Then play the game in **THIRSTY WORK**.

▼ On a cold day, warm water vapor in a bathroom condenses on the mirror. Water dribbles down the cold glass like rain.

Water and the weather

The weather is different all over the world. Water plays an important part in the weather, and it can appear in many forms.

▶ Tiny water droplets inside a **cloud** join together to become larger droplets. When they are big enough, the droplets fall out of the cloud as rain like these that have landed on a leaf.

▶ If the air near the ground has a lot of **water vapor** in it and is cooled, the water vapor **condenses** and forms a ground-level cloud. This is called **fog**.

◀ Sometimes it is very cold in a cloud, less than 32 °F (0°C). At this temperature, the water droplets in a cloud freeze together to form tiny crystals of **ice**. The crystals stick together and when the air below the cloud is also cold, the ice falls as **snow**.

◀ The air in a cloud is always moving. If an ice crystal is swept up through a cloud by rising winds, it can grow into a large ball of ice. This is how **hail** is formed. Sometimes hail can be huge. In 1970, a hailstone the size of a melon fell on Coffeyville, Kansas.

Water pressure

Have you ever tried to touch the bottom of a swimming pool? Sometimes when you try, you can feel the water pressing on your ears. This is because the water has a **pressure**, which is pushing on your eardrums. As you go deeper, the pressure gets greater and your ears may hurt.

Try holding your head at different angles. You can still feel the pressure of the water because it pushes in all directions. If you want to try this at home or at your swimming pool make sure that an adult or lifeguard is nearby.

▼ Seals always close up their nostrils and earholes when they dive deeply.

Experiment with water pressure

1. Ask an adult to help you make three holes at different heights down the side of a plastic bottle, using the point of some scissors. Get a friend to help you with the next part, because you need three hands.

2. With your friend, cover up the holes with your fingers and fill the bottle with water. Quickly take your fingers away. The water will spurt from the holes. Which hole has the biggest jet of water? Why do you think this is?

Making a submarine

Submarines are special ships that can travel underwater. They have to be strong so that the great **pressure** deep under the **ocean** does not crush them.

UNDERSEAS DEVELOP

It is easy to make a submarine that dives and surfaces just like the real thing. You can amaze your friends by making it go up and down without touching it – just like magic!

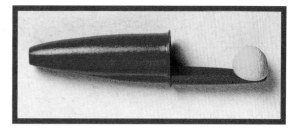

▲ All you need is a long, thin pen top, some modeling clay and a plastic bottle with a lid. Push a small blob of clay inside the pen top to block the hole and another small blob on the end. You may need to try different-sized blobs of clay.

▼ Put the top in a bottle full of water and screw the bottle lid on tightly. The pen top will float near the surface of the water.
   Now ask your friends if they want the pen top to **float** or **sink**. You can control it by squeezing the sides of the bottle!

DISK LINK
Join the Special Submergency Services and get equipped for underwater missions in **UNDER PRESSURE.**

ORP.

Weight and volume

About 2,200 years ago, the king of Syracuse in Sicily bought a golden crown. He was told that the crown was made of solid gold, but he wanted to make sure. The king asked a very clever man called Archimedes to check how much pure gold his crown was made of without harming it.

When he was getting into the bath, Archimedes suddenly realized how he could check the crown. He was so excited that he ran down the street. Unfortunately, he forgot to get dressed!

To check the king's crown, Archimedes first filled a basin with water. Then he dropped the crown in it and measured the change in the water level. This was the crown's **volume**. Archimedes weighed the crown and this volume of water, to find out how many times heavier the crown was than water. Then he compared the weight of solid gold with its volume in water to find out how much heavier gold is than water. He found that the crown was not solid gold after all!

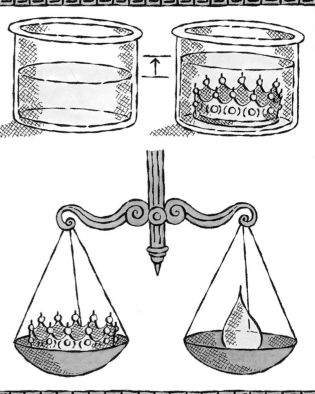

◀ Next time you take a bath, see what happens to the level of the water. Before you climb in, mark the top level of the water with a wax crayon. Now get into the bath and mark the new level. Look at the difference in height between the two marks. An object will push up the level of water by the amount of space it takes up, or its volume. You have just measured the volume of your body in the water!

Don't forget to wipe off the wax marks after the experiment!

Try this experiment to measure the volume of something a lot cheaper than a golden crown, such as a stone! Put exactly 500 ml of water into a measuring cup. Carefully put a stone into the cup and measure the new level of the water.

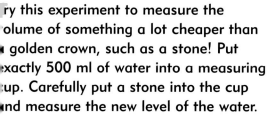

In this experiment, the water level rose from 500 ml to 600 ml. The stone took the place of 100 ml of water and pushed the level up.

One milliliter (1 ml) is the same as one cubic centimeter (1 cm³). So what was the volume of the stone?

Floating and sinking

Have you ever noticed that some things **float** and some things **sink**? Make a collection of things from around the house and guess which ones will float and which ones will sink.

▼ Fill a tank or bucket with water. Put your collection of things in the wate Were you surprised? Did you think that the heavy things would sink and the light ones float?

DISK LINK
Take the plunge! Discover more materials that float or sink in SINK OR SWIM.

Next time you go to a swimming pool try lifting a friend in the water. Your friend will feel much lighter than on land as the water gives support.

◀ Try **submerging** something that floats. You have to push to make it go underwater. How long does it take to rise up to the surface again?

▼ Fill a balloon or see-through plastic bag with water. Tell a friend that you can make it weigh nothing! Push the balloon underwater. It does not float or sink because it contains water, and so weighs the same as the water around it.

Shipshape and seaworthy

Ships and boats come in all shapes and sizes. See if you can design and make two different types of boats out of modeling clay.

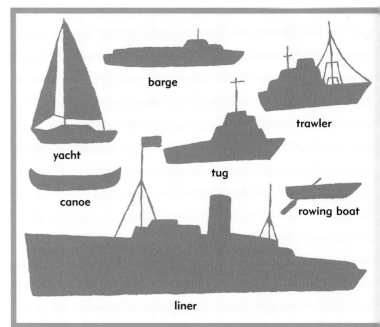

yacht

barge

trawler

canoe

tug

rowing boat

liner

▶ An **oil tanker** is a huge ship that carries crude oil. It has to hold a lot of oil and **float** in very shallow water in harbors. Look at this picture of an oil tanker. What do you notice about its shape?

◀ For a **yacht** to go fast, it must be very narrow to cut through the water. Try making a model yacht out of modeling clay with a straw mast and paper sail.

DISK LINK
Captain your own fleet of cargo ships in **ALL ABOARD**.

▼ Float your boat in the bath and blow on the sail. How can you make it go faster? See what happens if you change the shape of the sail and boat.

Surface tension

Something very odd happens to the surface of water. You have to get very close and look carefully to see it.

▶ How many pins at a time can you put in a glass filled to the brim with water, without any water spilling over? You may think the answer is none. Try it! Drop pins in one at a time. How many can you fit in the glass: 5, 10, 20, 40? Look closely at the surface of the water. Instead of pouring out, the water seems to be held in by an invisible "skin." This effect is called **surface tension**.

▶ You might be surprised to find out how strong the skin on the surface of water is. Do you think it can support a pin even though the pin is made of metal?
  Carefully **float** a small piece of paper towel on water. Quickly drop a pin on it and watch what happens when the paper towel **sinks**. The pin is left on the water's surface. If you look very closely, you should be able to see where the surface is holding it up.

Pins are very sharp, so be careful how you handle them!

▲ Some water insects, called pond skaters, can walk on water without getting their feet wet. Hairy pads on their legs trap bubbles of air and keep them afloat. Pond skaters can then move across the water's surface without breaking its "skin" and catch insects that have fallen into the water.

Separating colors

How black is black ink? Is it really made from a mix of different colors? This experiment shows you how to use water to find out. All you need is some white blotting paper, black ink, a glass, a pair of scissors and, of course, some water.

▲ Cut a circle out of the blotting paper a bit larger than the top of the glass. Put a small blot of ink in the center of the blotting paper. Next, make two cuts in it and fold the middle strip down. Carefully place the blotting paper over the top of the glass with the thin strip in the water. Watch closely and you won't believe your eyes!

As the water is slowly soaked up by the blotting paper, the ink separates into colors. This is called **chromatography**, which means "color drawing." Try it with different colored inks or food coloring to see what colors they are made of.

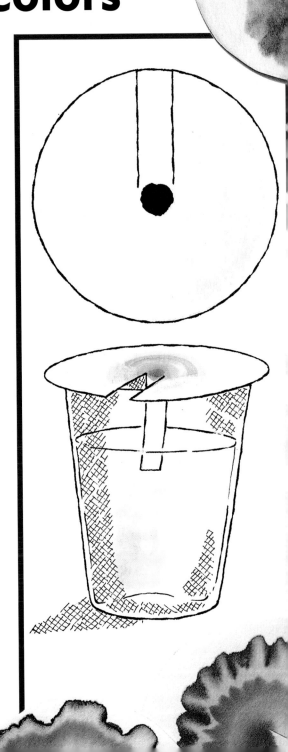

All-purpose water

We use water for all sorts of things around the house: washing, drinking, and watering plants. Wastewater from our households is cleaned at a sewage plant. How many uses for water can you think of?

To be sure of a good water supply to people's houses all year around, **dams** can be built across rivers to make artificial lakes called **reservoirs**. In wet weather the reservoirs fill up and store water for use when there is less rain. All over the world, reservoirs are also used to store water for **irrigation**. In areas where there is little rainfall, local farmers can channel water to their fields.

Water is a source of power, too. Try holding your thumb over the end of a hose with water flowing out of it. If you take your thumb away, the water will gush out. This water **force** is used in **hydroelectric power stations**.

◄ Watermills use the force of falling water. The rushing water of a stream pours along a special channel and onto the blades of a huge water wheel at the side of a mill. As the wheel turns, it powers machinery inside the mill that grinds huge stones together. In the past, these mills were used to crush corn into flour.

DISK LINK

Water is also used to put out fires. Put out a blaze in the water quiz, **FIREFIGHTER**.

◄ Dams store water in reservoirs high up in the mountains. Big pipes bring the water gushing downhill to hydroelectric power stations. There, the water rushes against the blades of a **turbine**. As the turbine spins quickly, it works the generator and makes the **electricity**.

► Falling water can be used to provide electricity to light whole cities.

Make your own water wheel

Here is an experiment to get power from moving water. You will need cardboard, an old thread spool, a straw, and some double-sided adhesive tape.

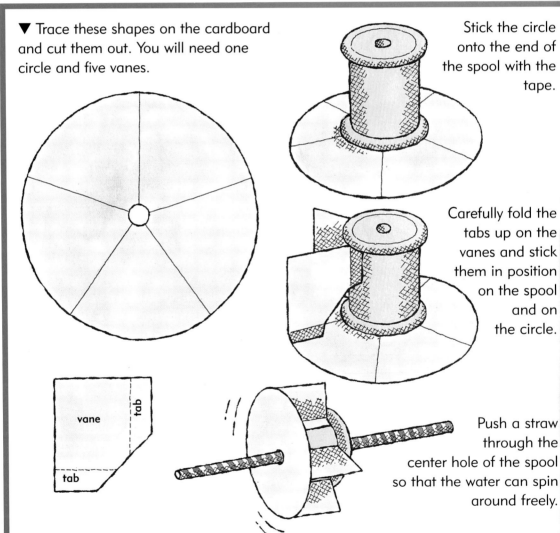

▼ Trace these shapes on the cardboard and cut them out. You will need one circle and five vanes.

Stick the circle onto the end of the spool with the tape.

Carefully fold the tabs up on the vanes and stick them in position on the spool and on the circle.

vane
tab
tab

Push a straw through the center hole of the spool so that the water can spin around freely.

◄ Try spinning the wheel in the kitchen sink under running water from the faucet. Where does it spin fastest? When it is near the spout or further down the stream of water? Why do you think this is? Where is the water moving fastest?

Being water aware

As the number of people on the earth increases, more and more clean water is needed. We must be careful not to waste our supply. The **rivers** and **lakes** where o clean water comes from have to be protected from **pollution**.

Harmful substances need to be removed from waste before it is poured into rivers or seas. At home, you can conserve the water supply by using less water and not flushing garbage down the drain. Cleaning wastewater to make it usable again is a long and expensive process.

DISK LINK
Play EVERY DROP
COUNTS to discover ways
to save water at home.

▶ Waste released from factories, and chemicals used in farming sometimes enter the water supply and cause pollution in rivers and **oceans**. This can make the water unhealthy for fish and other creatures.

◀ In some places around the world there is no regular supply of clean, running water, and there is a danger of water spreading disease. In many poorer countries where there is often less rainfall, water has to be carried home over long distances. Much of this water comes straight from rivers or deep wells.

Profile

Photocopy and fill in this water profile to keep a record of how much water you use every day. You will find it useful for the disk activity, EVERY DROP COUNTS.

How much do you drink each day? (All of these drinks are made up mostly of water.)

Canned or bottled drinks......... ☐

Glasses of water/milk/
soft drinks........................... ☐

Cups of tea/coffee/other
hot drinks............................ ☐

**How many times a day
do you brush your teeth?** ☐

**How many times a day
do you bathe?**

Sink.................................... ☐

Shower .... ☐

Bath.................................... ☐

**How many times a day
do you flush the toilet?** ☐

**How many times a week does
your family use a washing
machine?** ☐

**How many times a day does
your family wash dishes?** ☐

**Are they washed by hand or with
a dishwasher?**

....

**How many times a week is
water used to clean the house?** ☐

**Other possible uses. How many times
a month do you or your family...**

Wash a car............................ ☐

Water a garden .... ☐

Water indoor plants................ ☐

**Find out if you have a water
meter in your house and take
readings to see how much water
is used each week.**

Week 1...............................

Week 2...............................

Week 3...............................

Puzzles

Photocopy this page to write in your answers.

1. You have a measuring cup that holds 5 liters of water and a measuring cup that holds 4 liters of water. Use them to measure out exactly 3 liters. How do you do this?

2. Which of these is not like the others?

a) The Nile River

b) Loch Ness

c) Sea of Tranquility

d) Niagara Falls

e) The Suez Canal

3. Water word wheel

A lot of sports take place in water and on ice. How many can you find in the water wheel below? Do you know which are water sports and which are snow and ice sports?

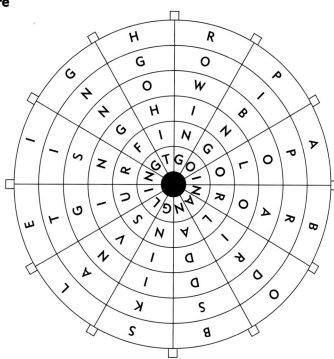

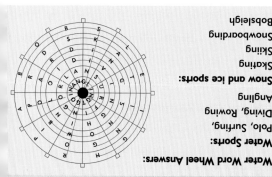

Glossary

Boiling: when a liquid turns into a gas by heating. Water boils at 212 °F (100 °C) at

sea level.

Chromatography: a way of separating a mixture to find out what it is made of.

Clouds: condensed water droplets or ice crystals that are held in the air.

Condensation: when a gas or vapor turns into a liquid by cooling.

Dam: an artificial blockage or wall holding back water.

Electricity: a type of energy used to light bulbs, turn motors, etc.

Energy: what things need to be active.

Evaporation: when a liquid turns into a gas or vapor.

Floating: resting on the surface of water.

Fog: condensed water droplets that float near the ground, making it difficult to see.

Force: the power to move an object.

Hail: small lumps of ice that fall from clouds.

Hydroelectric power station: a building where electricity is made by falling water pushed through turbines.

Ice: water that is frozen. Water freezes at 32 °F (0 °C) at sea level.

Irrigation: a way of moving water to dry areas using canals or ditches.

Lake: a large natural body of water.

Ocean: a huge body of salt water.

Oil tanker: a large ship used to carry oil.

Pollution: harmful substances that get into the environment.

Pressure: the weight of something on an area.

Reservoir: an artificially created lake.

River: water flowing over land and carving a channel for itself.

Sinking: falling toward the bottom in a liquid.

Snow: frozen water falling to the ground in crystals.

Steam: small water droplets in the air.

Submarine: a vessel that can go underwater.

Submerge: to sink below the water's surface.

Surface tension: the invisible "skin" on the surface of water.

Turbine: a spinning motor, pushed around by moving water or steam.

Volume: the space that something takes up.

Water cycle: the movement of water from the seas to the clouds, then to rain and rivers and back again.

Water vapor: water found in the atmosphere or air.

Weight: the force with which something pushes downward.

Yacht: a sailing boat built for cruising or racing.

Running your INTERFACT disk

Your INTERFACT CD-ROM will run on both PCs with Windows and on Apple Macs. To make sure that your computer meets the system requirements, check the list below.

SYSTEM REQUIREMENTS

PC
- Pentium 100 Mhz processor
- Windows 95, 98 (or later)
- 16 Mb RAM
- VGA 256-color monitor
- SoundBlaster-compatible soundcard
- 1 Mb Graphics card
- Double-speed CD-ROM drive

APPLE MACINTOSH
- 68020 processor minimum
  (PowerMac or G3/i-Mac recommended)
- System 7.0 (or later)
- 16 Mb RAM
- Color monitor set to at least 640 x
  480 pixels and 256 colors
- Double-speed CD-ROM drive

Loading your INTERFACT disk

INTERFACT is easy to load. You can run INTERFACT from the CD-ROM – you don't need to install it on your hard drive. But, before you begin, quickly run through the checklist below to ensure that your computer is ready to run the program.

PC WITH WINDOWS 95 OR 98

The program should start automatically when you put the disk in the CD-ROM drive. If it does not, follow these instructions.

1. Put the disk in the CD-ROM drive
2. Double-click MY COMPUTER
3. Double-click CD-ROM drive icon
4. Double-click on the WATER icon

APPLE MACINTOSH

1. Put the disk in the CD-ROM drive
2. Double-click on the INTERFACT icon
3. Double-click on the WATER icon

CHECKLIST

● First, make sure that your computer and monitor meet the system requirements as displayed on page 38.

● Ensure that your computer, monitor, and CD-ROM drive are all switched on and working normally.

● It is important that you do not have any other applications, such as word processors, running. Before starting INTERFACT, quit all other applications.

● Make sure that any screen savers for your computer have been switched off.

How to use INTERFACT

There are seven different features to explore. Use the controls on the right-hand side of the screen to select the one you want to play. You will see that the main area of the screen changes as you click on different features.

For example, this is what your screen will look like when you play SINK OR SWIM, in which you have to figure out which objects float and which sink. Once you've selected a feature, click on the main screen to start playing.

Now an apple will be dropped into the water. Do you think it will sink or float?

Click here t select the feature you want to pla

Click on the arrow keys to scroll through the different features on the disk or to find your way to the exit screen

DISK LINKS

When you read the book, you'll come across Disk Links. These show you where to find activities on the disk that relate to the page you are reading. Use the arrow keys to find the icon onscreen that matches the one in the Disk Link.

DISK LINK
Water is also used to put out fires. Put out a blaze in the water quiz, FIREFIGHTER.

BOOKMARKS

As you play the features on the disk, you'll bump into Bookmarks. These show you where to look in the book for more information about the topic onscreen. Just turn to the page of the book shown in the Bookmark.

23

ACTIVITIES

There are activities throughout this book, and on pages 34-35, there are puzzles and a profile to photocopy and fill in.

HOT DISK TIPS

● If you need help finding your way around the disk, click on the **?** icon to go to the HELP section.

● Any words that appear onscreen in a different color and underlined are "hot." This means that you can touch them with the cursor for more information or an explanation of the word.

● Keep a close eye on the cursor. When it changes from an arrow ↑ to a hand 🖐, click your mouse and something will happen.

● After you have chosen the feature you want to play, remember to move the cursor from the icon to the main screen before clicking your mouse again.

Troubleshooting

If you come across a problem loading or running the INTERFACT disk, you should find the solution here. If you still cannot solve your problem, call the helpline at 1-609-921-6700

YOUR COMPUTER SETUP

RESETTING SCREEN RESOLUTION

Resetting screen resolution in Windows 95 or 98:
Click on START at the bottom left of your screen, then click on SETTINGS, then CONTROL PANEL, then double-click on DISPLAY. Click on the SETTINGS tab at the top. Reset the Desktop area (or Display area) to 640 x 480 pixels and choose 256 colors, then click APPLY. You may need to restart your computer after changing display settings.

Resetting screen resolution for Apple Macintosh:
Click on the Apple symbol at the top left of your screen to access APPLE MENU ITEMS. Select CONTROL PANELS, then MONITORS (or MONITORS AND SOUND) then set the resolution to 640 x 480 and choose 256 colors. Screen resolutions can also be reset by clicking on the checkerboard symbol on the Control Strip.

ADJUSTING VIRTUAL MEMORY

Adjusting the Virtual Memory in Windows 95 or 98:
It is not recommended that these settings are adjusted as Windows will automatically configure your system as required.

Adjusting the Virtual Memory on Apple Macintosh:
If you have 16 Mb of RAM or more, WATER will run faster. If you do not have this amount of RAM free, hard disk memory can be used by switching on Virtual Memory. Select the Apple menu, Control Panels, then select Memory. Switch on Virtual Memory. Set the amount of memory you require, then restart your machine.

COMMON PROBLEMS

 Disk will not run
There is not enough memory available. Quit all other applications and programs. If this does not work, increase your machine's RAM by adjusting the Virtual Memory (see left).

 There is no sound (Try each of the following)

1. Ensure that your speakers or headphones are connected to the speaker outlet at the back of your computer. Make sure they are not plugged into the audio socket next to the CD-ROM drive at the front of the computer.

2. Ensure that the volume control is turned up (on your external speakers and by using internal volume control).

3. (PCs only) Your sound card is not SoundBlaster compatible. To make your settings SoundBlaster compatible, see your sound card manual for more information.

 Graphics do not load or are of poor quality
Not enough memory is available or you have the wrong display setting. Either quit other applications and programs or make sure that your monitor control is set to 256 colors.

 Graphics freeze or text boxes appear blank (Windows 95 or 98 only)
Graphics card acceleration is too high. Right-click your mouse on MY COMPUTER. Click on PROPERTIES, then PERFORMANCE, then GRAPHICS. Reset the hardware acceleration slider to "None." Click OK. Restart your computer.

 Text does not fit into boxes or hot words do not work (PCs only)
The standard fonts on your computer have been moved or deleted. You will need to reinstall the standard fonts for your computer. PC users require Arial. Please see your computer manual for further information.

 Printouts are not centered on the page or are partly cut off
Make sure that the page layout is set to "Landscape" in the Print dialog box.

 Your machine freezes
There is not enough memory available. Either quit other applications and programs or increase your machine's RAM by adjusting the Virtual Memory (see left).

Index

CD (PC/MAC) ISBN 1-58728-451-0

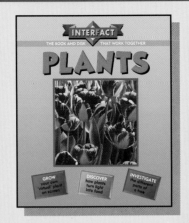

CD (PC/MAC) ISBN 1-58728-460-X

CD (PC/MAC) ISBN 1-58728-463-4

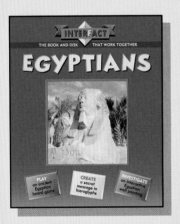

CD (PC/MAC) ISBN 1-58728-458-8

CD (PC/MAC) ISBN 1-58728-455-3

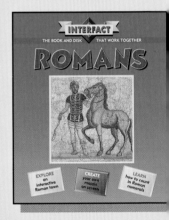

CD (PC/MAC) ISBN 1-58728-462-6

CD (PC/MAC) ISBN 1-58728-461-8

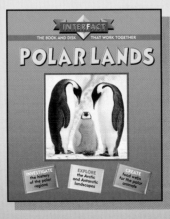

CD (PC/MAC) ISBN 1-58728-452-9

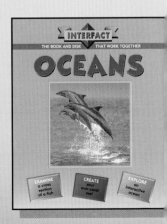

CD (PC/MAC) ISBN 1-58728-459-6

WATCH FOR NEW TITLES!

CD (PC/MAC) ISBN 1-58728-470-7

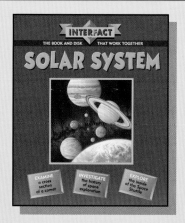

CD (PC/MAC) ISBN 1-58728-464-2

CD (PC/MAC) ISBN 1-58728-465-0

CD (PC/MAC) ISBN 1-58728-450-2

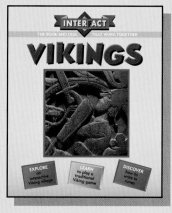

CD (PC/MAC) ISBN 1-58728-467-7

There is a wide array of **INTERFACT** titles to choose from, covering science, history, and nature.

And if you turn the page, you'll discover the new **INTERFACT REFERENCE** series of books and disk.

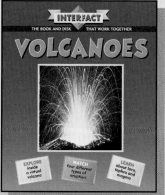
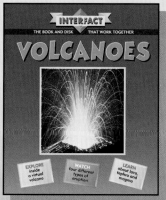

CD (PC/MAC) ISBN 1-58728-457-X

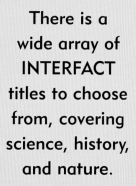

CD (PC/MAC) ISBN 1-58728-468-5

INTERFACT REFERENCE

Look for the new **INTERFACT REFERENCE** series.
Each large, colorful book works with an exciting disk, opening up
whole new areas of learning and providing a great reference source.

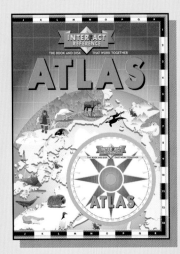

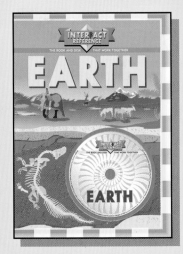

CD (PC/MAC) ISBN 1-58728-471-5   **CD** (PC/MAC) ISBN 1-58728-473-1   **CD** (PC/MAC) ISBN 1-58728-472-3

INTERFACT REFERENCE

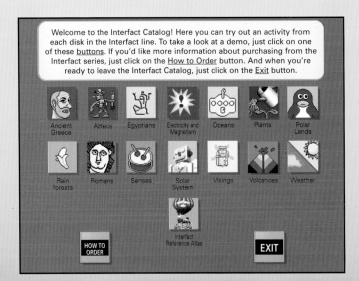

Welcome to the Interfact Catalog! Here you can try out an activity from each disk in the Interfact line. To take a look at a demo, just click on one of these buttons. If you'd like more information about purchasing from the Interfact series, just click on the How to Order button. And when you're ready to leave the Interfact Catalog, just click on the Exit button.

Make sure that you check out the INTERFACT Catalog on your INTERFACT CD-ROM.

You'll find a feature to play from each of the titles in the INTERFACT series.

For all orders or more information on other Two-Can books and multimedia contact.
Two-Can Publishing LLC, 234 Nassau Street, Princeton, NJ 08542
Call 1-609-921-6700, fax 1-609-921-3349 or visit our web site at
http://www.two-canpublishing.com